HOW TO USE YOUR LIGHTSABER

Your lightsaber toy is made up of two interlocking parts. Make sure the top and bottom parts are fully locked before you play with your toy. To light up your toy, move the switch on the handle to the right. Do not look into the light when your toy is ON. The handle also doubles as an image projector.

How to use your lightsaber as a projector:

- Twist and remove the green component from the handle of the lightsaber and set it aside.

- Starting with Disk 1, slide the picture disk into the slot as shown.

- Pick a clear space on a light-colored wall or ceiling three to five feet away. The biggest images can be seen when the projector is five feet from the wall or ceiling.

- Turn the projector ON.*

- Turn the disk to the right as you read through the story. The numbers next to the text correspond to the numbers on the projected images. Use the focusing ring at the end of the image projector to focus the pictures.

- Change disks as indicated in the story.

*Remember to turn the switch to OFF when not in use.

Interlocking Notch

Focusing Ring

Disk

Slot for Disk

ON/OFF Switch

STAR WARS®

EPISODE IV
A NEW HOPE

MOVIE THEATER
Storybook & Lightsaber Projector

Adapted by Benjamin Harper

studio fun

A READER'S DIGEST COMPANY

White Plains, New York • Montréal, Québec • Bath, United Kingdom

INTRODUCTION

A long time ago in a galaxy far, far away, the sinister Empire had taken control. Its grip was felt everywhere, the Emperor ruling with an iron fist and using the dark side of the Force. His second-in-command, Darth Vader, was his dreaded enforcer. Freedom fighters calling themselves the Rebel Alliance worked to topple the evil Empire. Princess Leia, Luke Skywalker, Han Solo, and all other members of the Rebellion fought endlessly to restore balance to the galaxy.

Darth Vader was chasing Princess Leia across the stars. Rebel spies had stolen plans to a secret Imperial space station called the Death Star. Princess Leia was trying to deliver them to the Rebellion so they could be analyzed and the station could be destroyed. But Darth Vader caught up to her.

DISK 1

Princess Leia stashed the plans into a droid called R2-D2. She ordered R2-D2 to flee in a pod and deliver the plans to a Jedi named Obi-Wan Kenobi on the planet Tatooine. R2-D2 and his friend C-3PO got into an escape pod and blasted off toward the planet.

Darth Vader and his stormtroopers ransacked the ship, but they couldn't find the plans. Vader took Princess Leia prisoner.

On Tatooine, Jawas captured R2-D2 and C-3PO and sold them to Luke Skywalker's uncle, Owen. As Luke was cleaning the droids, he found a message from Princess Leia that said Obi-Wan Kenobi was her only hope. Then Luke was called to dinner. When he got back, he discovered that R2-D2 had escaped! The droid had gone off on his own to look for Obi-Wan Kenobi.

The next day, Luke and C-3PO went to look for R2-D2. Sand People attacked Luke, but Obi-Wan Kenobi came to his rescue. Obi-Wan Kenobi told Luke that he had once been a Jedi Knight and had known Luke's father, who had been

killed by Darth Vader. Luke's father had been a student of Obi-Wan's and had asked Obi-Wan to give Luke his lightsaber when he was old enough.

Obi-Wan asked Luke to help him deliver R2-D2 and the stolen plans to rebel leaders on the planet Alderaan. Luke told Obi-Wan that he wanted to learn the ways of the Force—an energy field that flowed through and connected everything in the galaxy—and become a Jedi like his father had been.

They set out for Mos Eisley to find a star pilot. There they met Han Solo and his copilot, Chewbacca. Han needed a lot of money to pay off a crime lord named Jabba the Hutt, and Obi-Wan promised a large reward for his service. Han Solo agreed to take them to Alderaan.

Han Solo blasted his ship, the *Millennium Falcon*, out of Mos Eisley. He was chased by Star Destroyers but jumped to hyperspace toward Alderaan.

While they were traveling at light speed, Obi-Wan began training Luke Skywalker in the ways of the Force. Luke used his father's lightsaber for the very first time. Suddenly, Obi-Wan felt a disturbance in the Force and sensed that something terrible had happened.

When the crew jumped out of hyperspace, they discovered that Alderaan had been destroyed. They flew toward a small moon but found it was actually the Death Star—and it was pulling them in!

The crew hid in secret compartments aboard the *Millennium Falcon*. Then Luke and Han disguised themselves as stormtroopers. They snuck off the *Millennium Falcon* along with Obi-Wan and the droids to a command center on the Death Star. R2-D2 located the tractor beam that was holding them captive, and Obi-Wan went to turn off the beam.

R2 then discovered Princess Leia. Still wearing their stormtrooper armor and helmets, Han and Luke pretended that Chewbacca was a prisoner so they could get into the detention center and rescue the princess—but their plan was discovered. They were trapped! Stormtroopers rushed in and fired at them.

Princess Leia blasted a hole in a grate, and the group jumped into a trash compactor. But the compactor started closing in on them! Luke finally got through to C-3PO, who told R2 to plug into the Death Star's computer and turn off the compactor. With no time to spare, they were saved!

DISK 2

1

The heroes got out of the trash compactor and headed back toward the *Millennium Falcon*.

Meanwhile, Obi-Wan managed to turn off the tractor beam. But one task remained—he had to face Darth Vader. Vader, at one time a Jedi, had turned to the dark side of the Force. During the lightsaber battle between Obi-Wan and Vader, Obi-Wan Kenobi sacrificed himself so his friends could escape.

The heroes ran toward the ship as stormtroopers rushed after them. Luke fired his blaster at the troopers, and the rebels managed to escape.

The *Millennium Falcon* soared out of the Death Star. Once the ship was free, Han and Luke fought off TIE fighters in a space battle before zooming to the rebel base on Yavin 4.

However, Darth Vader had placed a homing beacon on their ship and was tracking them, so the Death Star could locate and destroy the rebel base!

The rebels analyzed the plans delivered by Princess Leia and found a weakness in the Death Star! Proton torpedoes shot into an exhaust port would cause the space station to explode. It was their only chance.

As Luke volunteered to fly into battle, Han decided to leave. He had other business to take care of and thought the rebels had no chance of winning.

The rebel pilots boarded their X-wing and Y-wing fighters and shot off toward the Death Star.

The rebels attacked the Death Star, but TIE fighters were ready to strike! They swarmed the rebel pilots and a great battle ensued.

Darth Vader flew into combat alongside the stormtroopers. Luke Skywalker zoomed into a trench on the Death Star to launch his proton torpedoes. As he raced toward the exhaust port, Obi-Wan spoke to him through the Force. He listened. He focused.

He approached the port and just as Darth Vader was about to fire on him, Han Solo flew in and fired. Darth Vader spiraled out of control and Luke made his shot. It went in and the Death Star exploded!

(3)

The surviving rebels flew back to Yavin 4, and Darth Vader soared into space.

(4)

After the Battle of Yavin, the Rebel Alliance held a ceremony for the heroes. Luke Skywalker, Han Solo, and Chewbacca were all honored. Princess Leia awarded medals to Luke and Han for their service to the Rebellion. As they stood, the entire Rebel Alliance cheered.

GENERAL SAFETY AND CARE

- Non-rechargeable batteries are not to be recharged.
- Different types of batteries or new and used batteries are not to be mixed.
- Batteries are to be inserted with the correct polarity.
- Exhausted batteries are to be removed from the toy.
- The supply terminals are not to be short-circuited.
- Do not mix old and new batteries.
- Do not mix alkaline, standard (carbon-zinc), or rechargeable (nickel-cadmium) batteries.
- Prevent the book and unit from getting wet and avoid exposure to excessively hot or cold temperatures.
- Rechargeable batteries are only to be charged under adult supervision.
- Rechargeable batteries are to be removed from the toy before being charged.
- Remove batteries when not in use or discharged.

BATTERY INFORMATION

To remove or insert replaceable batteries, remove the safety screw from battery compartment door. Lift and remove door. Take out and safely dispose of old batteries. Follow polarity diagram inside battery compartment to insert three new batteries of any of the following types: AG13 or equivalent. Alkaline batteries are recommended. Put battery compartment door back and secure safety screw. Do not use excess force or an improper type or size screwdriver.

CAUTION

To ensure proper safety and operation, battery replacement must always be done by an adult. Never let a child use this product unless battery door is secure. Batteries are small objects and could be ingested. Keep all batteries away from small children and immediately dispose of any used batteries safely. Projector is not a viewer. Do not look into the lens when light is on.